Note to parents, carers and teachers

Read it yourself is a series of modern stories, favourite characters and traditional tales written in a simple way for children who are learning to read. The books can be read independently or as part of a guided reading session.

Each book is carefully structured to include many high-frequency words vital for first reading. The sentences on each page are supported closely by pictures to help with understanding, and to offer lively details to talk about.

The books are graded into four levels that progressively introduce wider vocabulary and longer stories as a reader's ability and confidence grows.

Ideas for use

- Begin by looking through the book and talking about the pictures. Has your child heard this story before?

- Help your child with any words he does not know, either by helping him to sound them out or supplying them yourself.

- Developing readers can be concentrating so hard on the words that they sometimes don't fully grasp the meaning of what they're reading. Answering the puzzle questions at the end of the book will help with understanding.

For more information and advice on Read it yourself and book banding, visit **www.ladybird.com/readityourself**

Book Band 4

Level 1 is ideal for children who have received some initial reading instruction. Each story is told very simply, using a small number of frequently repeated words.

Special features:

man

pig

woman

hen

cat

boys

dog

big pancake

Opening pages introduce key story words

Just then, the big pancake saw a deep river.

"Help!" said the big pancake.

"I will help you," said a pig. "Come here and jump on."

Large, clear type

Careful match between story and pictures

Educational Consultant: Geraldine Taylor
Book Banding Consultant: Kate Ruttle

LADYBIRD BOOKS

UK | USA | Canada | Ireland | Australia
India | New Zealand | South Africa

Ladybird Books is part of the Penguin Random House group of companies
whose addresses can be found at global.penguinrandomhouse.com.

www.penguin.co.uk   www.puffin.co.uk   www.ladybird.co.uk

Penguin
Random House
UK

First published 2014
This edition published 2014
001

Copyright © Ladybird Books Ltd, 2014

Printed in China

A CIP catalogue record for this book is available from the British Library

ISBN: 978-0-72328-047-7

All correspondence to:
Ladybird Books
Penguin Random House Children's
80 Strand, London WC2R 0RL

The
Big Pancake

Illustrated by Emilie Chollat

man

hen

pig

cat

boys

6

woman

big
pancake

dog

7

A woman had seven little boys.

The seven little boys were very hungry.

The woman made a pancake.
It was a very big pancake!

"We will eat it up!" said the
seven little boys.

11

But the big pancake jumped up and ran away.

"Stop! We are very hungry!" said the woman.

The big pancake
did not stop.

A hungry man saw the
big pancake.

"I will eat you up," said the
man. But the big pancake
ran on.

Next, a hungry cat saw
the big pancake.

"Come here! I will eat you,"
said the hungry cat. But the
big pancake did not stop.

Then, a hungry dog saw
the big pancake.

"Stop! I will eat you up,"
said the dog. But the big
pancake did not stop.
It just ran away.

Next, a hungry hen saw the big pancake.

"Come here! I will eat you all up," said the hungry hen. But the big pancake just ran away.

Just then, the big
pancake saw a deep river.

"Help!" said the big pancake.

"I will help you," said
a pig. "Come here
and jump on."

"Help! The river is too deep," said the big pancake.

"Come on," said the pig. "Jump up here."

"The river is too deep," said the big pancake. "Help!"

"Just jump up here," said the pig.

But the pig was a very
hungry pig.

"Snap! Snap!" said the pig.
And the pig had all the
big pancake!

How much do you remember about the story of The Big Pancake? Answer these questions and find out!

- How many little boys does the woman have?

- Can you name at least one character who chases the big pancake?

- Who says they will help the big pancake?

Look at the pictures from the story and say the order they should go in.

A

B

C

D

Tick the books you've read!

Level 1

Level 2

Level 3

Level 4